WHAT A WONDERFUL WORLD

For Alice and Ben,
may the world always fill you with wonder – L.S-S

To everyone across the world, big or small, who works to make a better tomorrow – L.H.

DURRELL

The publisher would like to give special thanks to Durrell Wildlife Conservation Trust and Lee Durrell for their valuable contribution to this book.

To find out more about Durrell Wildlife Conservation Trust and the wildlife projects it supports, visit **www.durrell.org**

A TEMPLAR BOOK

First published in the UK in 2021 by Templar Books,
an imprint of Bonnier Books UK,
4th Floor, Victoria House,
Bloomsbury Square,
London WC1B 4DA
www.bonnierbooks.co.uk

ISBN 978-1-78741-877-6

This book was typeset in Sofa Sans, Otari and Origo.
The illustrations were created digitally.

The publisher would like to thank all of the people who have shared their knowledge, experiences and voices to help create this book.

Written by Leisa Stewart-Sharpe
Consultant Sophie Stafford
Edited by Carly Blake
Designed by Olivia Cook, Ted Jennings and Nathalie Eyraud
Production Controller Ché Creasey

Printed in Latvia

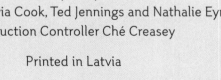

MIX
Paper from responsible sources
FSC® C002795
www.fsc.org

This book is forest-friendly!
The FSC logo means the paper in this book comes from sustainable forests, helping to ensure our forests are alive for generations to come.

WHAT A WONDERFUL WORLD

templar
books

CONTENTS

FOREWORD FROM
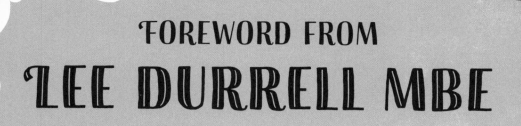
LEE DURRELL MBE

Humans are now the greatest force of nature and it's not all good for the planet. We constantly hear about the destruction of the natural world, the changing climate and the extinction of species, but there are humans taking positive actions that are starting to tip the balance. In this book these people are known as Earth Shakers.

To make a positive change, first you must care *about* our planet, and then you will take care *of* our planet. I started caring about the Earth when I was a child, by spending time walking in the woods, listening to birdsong and sketching wild flowers – in other words, I was connecting with nature. I started taking care of it when I was ten years old, and it was a moment I will remember forever. Two huge old oak trees in front of our house had to be cut down so that the road could be widened. I cried and cried, but then I found some acorns next to the trunks of the felled giants. I planted them nearby, so that they could one day grow into oak trees. I have been 'planting acorns' ever since.

As the number of Earth Shakers grows every day – and I hope you count yourselves among them – there is good reason to believe that many generations to come will still enjoy the amazing variety of life in our wonderful world.

Lee Durrell MBE

**Honorary Director,
Durrell Wildlife Conservation Trust**

About Lee Durrell and Durrell Wildlife Conservation Trust

American zoologist Lee Durrell married author and founder of Jersey Zoo, Gerald Durrell, in 1979. Together they spent 15 years writing and making television programmes about natural history and conservation. Lee also worked on a number of conservation projects led by Durrell Wildlife Conservation Trust, notably in Madagascar. Succeeding Gerald as Honorary Director of the Trust, Lee maintains a deep interest in her late husband's legacy and received an MBE for services to conservation in 2011.

In 1963 Gerald Durrell set up a conservation charity to oversee the activities of Jersey Zoo and to undertake conservation around the world to fulfil its mission to save species from extinction. Durrell Wildlife Conservation Trust works with hundreds of species in dozens of countries. It has trained thousands of conservationists and has embarked on an ambitious programme to rewild ten ecosystems and better connect a million people to nature.

OUR WONDERFUL WORLD

Earth – third rock from the Sun, wrapped in gas, covered in water and crawling with life. It's our oasis among the stars and nearly eight billion humans, and countless plant and animal species, call this planet home. It's the only planet we've got, and, boy oh boy, did we get lucky!

'OUR WORLD IS AWE-INSPIRING

Earth is a place of giant proportions. There are over one million mountains, many with ragged summits that peak beyond the clouds. The world's forests span almost 40 million square kilometres – enough to cover Australia five times over. As for the ocean, it wraps around more than 70 per cent of the world, an area 36 times bigger than the United States.

'OUR WORLD IS MYSTERIOUS

Although we have explored much of the planet, there are still mysteries waiting to be uncovered. Believe it or not, more than 80 per cent of the ocean is unmapped, and scientists believe we have laid eyes on less than 15 per cent of the world's species. Incredibly, around 15,000 species of living things are discovered every year. Some you have to see to believe, such as the colourful species of peacock spider discovered in 2015, nicknamed 'sparklemuffin'. It has a mesmerising, leg-waving dance!

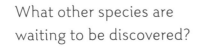

What other species are waiting to be discovered?

'BUT ABOVE ALL ELSE, OUR WORLD IS WONDERFUL

Colourful coral reefs, untamed jungles, great white polar wildernesses, snaking rivers, vast grasslands, scorching deserts and towering mountains make Earth unlike any other planet we know of. Each habitat teems with its own unique species, living together in ecosystems perfectly balanced by nature.

Every inch of Earth is a reminder of why this precious planet is worth protecting, and it needs us now more than ever before . . .

HOW WE CHANGED THE WORLD

Stare into a churning sea, a raging storm or the boiling crater of a volcano, and you need no reminder that there are great forces at work on our planet. Yet in the 200,000 years that modern humans have walked the Earth, WE have become the greatest force of nature the world has ever known. Just a couple of hundred years ago we set a big change in motion.

In the late 1700s the Industrial Revolution began in Britain and quickly spread to other parts of the world. We invented factories and new machines powered by coal, oil and gas. These substances are known as fossil fuels and when burned they release carbon dioxide gas (CO_2) into the atmosphere. After factories came cars and, later, aeroplanes – inventions that revolutionised travel, but pumped even more CO_2 into the air from their engines. Today, we produce enough CO_2 to fill more than 1,000 two-storey homes every second.

GLOBAL WARMING

As well as CO_2, our activities have released another gas into the atmosphere. Landfill – the rubbish we bury in the ground – and livestock farming create methane. Methane and CO_2 are known as 'greenhouse gases'. These gases stop some of the Sun's heat escaping back into space and cause what is known as 'the greenhouse effect' – like how the glass in a greenhouse traps the warmed air inside when the Sun shines down. The greenhouse effect is what makes Earth a good place for life, but the amount of greenhouse gases we have added to the atmosphere is causing the planet to warm faster than at any other time in human history.

'ONE DEGREE

Earth is about one degree Celsius hotter since the Industrial Revolution began. One degree may not sound like much, but it is enough to melt polar sea ice and glaciers, cause sea levels to rise, make the weather more extreme and change climates around the world.

'WE MADE OURSELVES AT HOME

To make matters worse, we have cut down three trillion trees, made enough concrete to thinly pave the planet's entire surface and filled the ocean with tiny plastic pieces. According to scientists, our actions have helped set in motion a mass extinction that is seeing wildlife disappear at a faster rate than ever before, with many species disappearing even before they are discovered.

It's scary to read, but this is not the end of our story.
It's the beginning of a new chapter . . .

9

THE EARTH SHAKERS ARE RISING

Our planet is under pressure, but it's not too late to make things right. We have changed the world before and we can change the world once more, this time with a little help from Earth Shakers – people all around the world taking action and making changes for a healthier future.

From young people marching in the streets, and scientists and conservationists living in wild corners of our planet, to primary school students tending beehives, planting trees and cleaning up their neighbourhoods, Earth Shakers everywhere are standing up for nature.

SKOLSTREJK FÖR KLIMATET

Already, positive changes can be seen all around us. We can drive electric cars and power our homes using energy created by water, the wind and the Sun, instead of by burning fossil fuels. Conservation projects have helped to save extraordinary species from extinction, such as the giant panda and humpback whale, and protect huge areas of land and ocean from human development. Although there is still much more to do, more and more Earth Shakers are rising to the challenge. They are clever, caring and capable of incredible things.

They are just like you.

First, let's meet the people studying Earth to see what's happening . . .

EARTH IS SENDING US A MESSAGE

Thanks to satellites, drones and scientific advancements, we have been able to study, observe and record our planet in more detail than ever before. Not only does data show us the changes that are happening, but we can also feel, see and hear the changes all around us. The Earth Shakers who study the planet help us understand what's happening now and what could happen in the future.

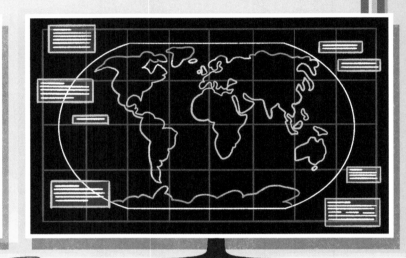

WE CAN FEEL THE WEATHER CHANGING

Our warming planet is changing the weather and, in some cases, making it more extreme. When an extreme weather event occurs, such as a heatwave, bushfire or flood, climate scientist Dr Friederike Otto at the University of Oxford wants to find out if human-made climate change made that bad weather worse. She makes a climate model – a digital copy of our world and its weather, created inside a huge supercomputer. By changing the amount of greenhouse gases in the climate model to the level it was before we started to burn lots of fossil fuels and comparing it with today's warmer world, Fredi can see what these changes mean for people and for wildlife.

"If we continue to burn coal, gas and oil, Earth will continue to warm, and what now feels like a really hot summer will seem like a cool summer very soon."

"Nature isn't something that only happens in the middle of the countryside – it's right in front of us. We are part of it – and urgently need to look up, listen, and get on nature's wavelength so we can save it."

WE CAN HEAR IT IN THE SILENT SPACES

The world's wild spaces are falling silent, as a growing number of bird species are threatened with extinction, including puffins, snowy owls and turtle doves. Naturalist David Lindo fears children today will never know the turtle dove's distinctive purring song, which was once a sound of the British summer. Turtle dove numbers have fallen by around 80 per cent since 1980. Each year, they migrate more than 5,000 kilometres from wintering grounds in Africa back to their breeding grounds in Europe, but millions of birds are shot down by hunters. The birds that successfully complete the journey find the woodlands where they breed increasingly cleared for farming.

'WE CAN SEE THE OCEAN CHANGING

On Australia's Great Barrier Reef, marine biologist Professor Terry Hughes investigates what warmer oceans mean for the health of coral reefs. Healthy coral reefs can be a rainbow of brilliant colours, but many are turning white. Corals get their bright colours from algae called zooxanthellae (*zoo-zan-thell-ee*) that live inside their tissues. When the ocean gets too hot, zooxanthellae get stressed and stop feeding the coral. This makes the coral turn white in a process called coral bleaching. If water temperatures drop within a few weeks, zooxanthellae will recover, and the coral's colour will return. But if not, the coral will starve and die.

"If global warming goes beyond 1.5 degrees Celsius, fragile branching corals will disappear, along with fish that live in their nooks and crannies. Only big mound corals will survive, and the reef will become flatter with fewer species."

Take a journey around the world, from the highest mountain peaks, down into the blue ocean, and meet some of the Earth Shakers who have helped change our planet for the better . . .

ON THE ROOF OF THE WORLD
MOUNTAINS

Mountains are mighty barriers of rock covering around 25 per cent of Earth's land surface. Born when continental plates collide, carved by giant glaciers and sculpted by wind and rain, mountains are breathtaking monuments to powerful forces at work on our planet.

At high altitude, the weather can change in minutes, from clear skies to blizzards and sunshine to sub-zero temperatures. Fast-moving masses of snow with the weight of three Empire State Buildings can roar down the slopes as avalanches. Although mountains are one of the most dangerous and unforgiving environments on our planet, around 1 in 10 people and a variety of species live in these regions.

Huge, shaggy-furred yaks are at home in the thin air and bitter winds experienced at elevations beyond 5,000 metres.

THE DEATH ZONE

The higher you go, the harder life becomes. Areas with an altitude higher than 8,000 metres have so little oxygen no plants or animals can survive. Only 14 mountains on Earth have peaks higher than 8,000 metres – that's about 10 times higher than the world's tallest building, the Burj Khalifa in Dubai. Ten are in the Himalayas, and the highest – Mount Everest – towers 8,850 metres above sea level.

LIFE ON THE EDGE

At around 3,500 metres on the Himalayan slopes, trees give way to smaller plants and shrubs, which are grazed on by one of the world's toughest animal mountaineers – the spiral-horned markhor. Beyond 4,000 metres, tough, low-growing plants, such as grasses and mosses, peek from between rocks, and are nibbled on by little Himalayan marmots. High up on rocky outcrops, spotted snow leopards scan for prey where large, woolly, goatlike tahrs scramble over ridges. Beyond 6,000 metres, Himalayan jumping spiders pounce on insects blown up on the wind.

CLEAN MOUNTAIN AIR

The easier it becomes to access the world's mountains, the more people come to visit, leaving a trail of rubbish behind. But in mountain valleys, a different kind of pollution has taken hold – air pollution. In areas that are largely surrounded by mountains, the wind is blocked and air pollution cannot blow away – this is called the 'basin effect'. In more than 400 of America's national parks – many of which are in mountainous regions – air pollution has reached unhealthy levels.

But at the foot of the Himalayas, the winds of change are blowing . . .

PRITI SAKHA
FIGHTING FOR CLEAN AIR

Priti Sakha lives in the ancient city of Bhaktapur, Nepal, at the foot of Mount Everest. She used to be able to watch the Sun rise over the mountains, but air pollution here is now some of the worst on Earth. Across the city, old cars and motorbikes, open fires used to burn waste and brick-making ovens called kilns pump toxic fumes into the air. Like a thick, grey quilt, a layer of smog blankets the city and nearby towns.

Priti loves Bhaktapur. It's where she was born, and she doesn't want to go anywhere else, but the air is choking people, trees are being cut down, and the once narrow road from Bhaktapur to Kathmandu is now a highway.

"The air burns our eyes and makes it hard to breathe. I felt like I was putting my life at risk to get an education."

People are encouraged to stay off the streets early in the mornings, when the air is at its worst, but that was when Priti needed to travel to college in Kathmandu to study environmental science. Determined to help her local community, at the age of 19, Priti used what she had learned to volunteer in the Nepalese Youth for Climate Action group (NYCA). She took part in street clean-ups and protests, encouraging people to be aware and responsible for the waste and pollution they produce. Priti also visited schools as a volunteer to speak to students and adults, to help them understand the dangers of air pollution and how everyone can work towards a cleaner future in the Himalayas. A future where her father no longer has to wear a mask to the factory where he works and where the air no longer causes elderly people and children to suffer from asthma.

'GREEN' TIP

Grow some house plants! They absorb toxins and pollutants in the air that can give you a headache, make you dizzy or irritate your eyes.

Thanks to Priti and many other volunteers, the NYCA's school awareness programme has spread the message to thousands of students so far. They continue the important work of helping people discover it is within their power to protect the mountains they love.

"I want to talk to people and make them aware of what's happening to our world. The mountains are our pride. I'm taking a stand."

Nepalese Youth for Climate Action

NYCA

Caring for Climate   Caring for ourselves

The Himalayas were once glorious white mountains, but hotter summers have melted a quarter of their ice. Global warming has also weakened the monsoon – the strong winds that often bring heavy rain that forms snow.

KAMIKATSU TOWN
JAPAN'S ZERO-WASTE WARRIORS

Perched on a mountainside on the Japanese island of Shikoku, the small town of Kamikatsu thinks waste is RUBBISH! The town's 1,500 residents used to burn what they threw away or bury it in the ground, but today they recycle almost all of their rubbish, sorting their waste into not two, not three, but 45 different categories! Food waste is composted, tin cans and plastic bottles are washed and dried, paper and cardboard are sorted into bundles, then everything is taken down to Kamikatsu's Zero Waste Center where old becomes new again.

Recycling is sent away, including cooking oil, which is used to make fertiliser. At the Kuru Kuru (meaning 'circular') shop, clothes, crockery and ornaments are given back into the community, turning one person's trash into someone else's treasure. Creative grandmas even upcycle old kimonos and *koinobori* (fish-shaped flags flown across Japan on Children's Day) into teddy bears, bags and clothes. More than 10 tonnes are brought into the Kuru Kuru shop each year, and almost the same amount is given back to the community.

It's estimated that by 2025, the world's cities will create 2 billion tonnes of waste each year – that's 1.4 kilograms per person per day, the same weight as 100 empty drink cans. The town of Kamikatsu may be small, but it has shown the world that we can all strive to be 'zero heroes'.

KURU
KURU

"We are the ones who decide what waste is, so we are the ones who can change it!"

'GREEN' TIP

Give old books, clothes and other items you no longer want a second chance at life by organising a swap party with your friends.

SARAH-LOUISE ADAMS
A FROG'S FAIRY TALE

The critically endangered mountain chicken frog, one of the world's biggest frogs, is only found on the mountainous Caribbean islands of Dominica and Montserrat. On Montserrat, frog numbers had reduced due to loss of habitat from volcanic activity and being hunted for food. Then, in 2009, the deadly frog-killing chytrid (*kit-rid*) fungus arrived. That's when biologist Sarah-Louise Adams and the team at Durrell Wildlife Conservation Trust leapt into action.

Fifty mountain chicken frogs were airlifted to Europe, to Durrell's zoo in Jersey, UK, as well as zoos in London and Sweden, to begin a breeding programme. Staying on Montserrat, Sarah-Louise began treating the remaining frogs infected with chytrid. Every week for six months, she bathed them to clean the fungus away. Although the treated frogs were living longer, they were still slowly disappearing. Suddenly, in early 2010, a volcanic eruption covered the frogs' home in ash and forced Sarah-Louise to evacuate. As time went on, only two frogs remained – a male and a female living 900 metres apart.

"Even if it was a happy ending for our frog prince and princess, we knew we had to do more to make absolutely sure the species survived."

Later that year Sarah-Louise returned to Montserrat with 64 healthy young frogs from Europe to help rebuild the population. This time the frogs were fitted with radio transmitters, and Sarah and the team tracked their movements each night. Close monitoring and study of the rare mountain chicken frog continues today, helping its chances of survival by finding new ways to fight the deadly fungus.

'GREEN' TIP

Encourage frogs and other amphibians into your garden by making a wildlife-friendly pond. Add plenty of logs and stones to help frogs get in and out.

THE LUNGS OF THE WORLD
RAINFORESTS

As the Sun rises over the rainforest, nature's alarm clock begins to sound – a chorus of frogs chirping, birds singing and insects humming signals another busy day is beginning in the jungle.

Tropical rainforests grow close to the equator, sandwiched between the tropic of Capricorn and the tropic of Cancer. Here, temperatures are warm and there is a lot of rain – between 2 and 10 metres a year! Temperate rainforests grow further north and south in cooler coastal areas. Together, tropical and temperate rainforests cover around three per cent of Earth's surface, yet bustle with over half of the world's land species.

Africa's Congo rainforest is the world's second-largest tropical forest. It teems with an incredible variety of life – including 10,000 plant species, 400 mammal species and 1,000 bird species – much of which is found nowhere else on Earth.

LIFE IN LAYERS

Life thrives in every layer of Africa's Congo rainforest. High up in the emergent layer, where the tallest trees break through, food and light are plentiful, but only the most expert climbers and flyers live here. Crowned eagles hunt monkeys and snakes, and take to the sky when they are ready to strike.

The thick canopy below is home to more animal life than any other layer. Johanna's sunbirds flit from tree to tree and rare orchids bloom like jungle jewels. Bonobo monkeys 'hoot' to each other – it pays to make a racket so your neighbours know you are nearby.

Small, young trees make up the steamy understorey. Here, a Johnston's three-horned chameleon basks in the sun and a hungry leopard waits up on a branch for a small antelope, called a duiker, to wander by.

On the gloomy forest floor endangered mountain gorillas, forest elephants and rare okapis (or forest giraffes) feed on leaves, stems and fruits. But for every animal you see, many more lurk underfoot in the decaying leaf litter, including the African baboon spider.

OUR VANISHING LEAF LINE

Rainforests have been here for at least 180 million years but they are disappearing in the blink of an eye. An area of rainforest as big as the UK is lost each year, and in the Amazon alone, a patch the size of three football pitches disappears every day. At this rate, rainforests will be gone within 100 years.

But our Earth Shakers are planting the seeds of change . . .

FELIX FINKBEINER
MAKING EARTH GREEN AGAIN

In 2007, nine-year-old schoolboy Felix Finkbeiner was learning about the climate crisis at school in Germany, when he had a BIG idea that grew into something wonderful.

"Let's plant one million trees in every country on Earth!"

His class thought it was a great idea, but to grow big you have to start small. A few months later Felix planted his first tree, a crab apple, at school. Other local schools quickly heard about Felix's tree-planting plans and a year later 50,000 tree seedlings had been planted across Germany. Inspired by the huge support for his project, Felix set up the Plant-for-the-Planet organisation to help more children around the world to plant trees. Today, with a little help from the United Nations, an army of more than 91,000 children in 75 countries have joined in.

Trees are one of the best ways to tackle climate change. They are our planet's lungs, drawing in CO_2 from pollution and breathing out, it's estimated, over a quarter of the world's oxygen (O_2).

"Before humans, Earth had six trillion trees but today only three trillion are left. If we can plant a trillion trees it will buy us enough time to combat the climate crisis and keep global temperature rises below two degrees."

In 2015, Plant-for-the-Planet began a huge reforestation project in Mexico. The Maya Forest on the Yucatán Peninsula is the second-largest tropical rainforest in the Americas, after the Amazon, but each year an area the size of New York City is slashed and burned to make room for farms. When forests are destroyed in this way they release CO_2 back into the air, making the planet warmer.

A team of 100 volunteers works over an area of forest around the size of 30,000 football pitches, planting a tree every 15 seconds. Seeds have been carefully selected by hand, sown in the best soil, and each young tree looked after in a tree nursery until it is ready to be planted.

Already eight million new trees have grown on the Yucatán and Felix aims to have planted 100 million new trees by 2029 – 50 for every person on the peninsula. Across the world, more than 15 billion trees (and counting!) have been planted in over 200 countries. As Felix says, it's time to stop talking and start planting.

'GREEN' TIP

You can help balance out your carbon emissions (this is called offsetting) by planting a tree as part of Felix's Trillion Tree Campaign.

On the Yucatán, trees grow four times faster than in Europe, making it the perfect place to plant.

DR PETER PRATJE
GRANDFATHER OF THE ORANGUTAN

On the Indonesian island of Sumatra, deep in the Bukit Tigapuluh rainforest, wildlife biologist Dr Peter Pratje has spent over 20 years living and working with orangutans. Each morning branches crack overhead, flashes of orange fur move through the trees and bellowing calls echo out – the orangutans have arrived for 'jungle school'.

A century ago, around 230,000 of these great apes called the islands of Sumatra and Borneo home, but today they are endangered – in Sumatra, around 13,000 orangutans remain. Their rainforest homes are disappearing, cleared or burned to make way for oil palm crops. Young orangutans are separated from their mothers and become orphans. Thankfully, at jungle school, these orphans get a second chance to return to the forest.

"As a child, I dreamed about living in the jungle. As a student, I got to do it, studying orangutan conservation in Indonesia. In 1998 when I heard that someone was needed to run a jungle school in Sumatra, I leapt at the chance!"

At 10am the school day starts and the orangutans get piggybacks into the forest. Here, they learn by doing and imitating. Peter and his volunteers show them how to climb trees, build sleeping nests, peel back the bark to eat vines and open up termite mounds to get at the tasty insects – everything their mother would have shown them. When the apes are old and smart enough, they can be released. Known as 'the orangutan grandfather', Peter has helped more than 170 orphaned orangutans return to life in the wild.

'GREEN' TIP

Write to your local supermarket and ask that the products it sells only use sustainable palm oil, grown in a way that doesn't destroy the rainforests.

ANGONOKA GUARDIANS
MADAGASCAR'S TORTOISE PATROL

Around 200,000 species of plants and animals that live on the island of Madagascar are found nowhere else on Earth, including one of the world's rarest tortoises – the ploughshare, known locally as 'angonoka'. This animal would already be extinct were it not for its bodyguards – the angonoka guardians.

The ploughshare tortoise lives in one remote corner of Madagascar's bamboo scrublands, but over many years its home has been cleared for grazing land and plantations, pushing it to the brink of extinction. Working with conservationists and the local government for over 30 years, the Malagasy people have supported a breeding programme to reintroduce the slow-growing ploughshare into the protected Baly Bay National Park.

"But no sooner are the ploughshares released, they're stolen."

As animals become rare, they become valuable to criminals. With its beautiful golden shell, a ploughshare can sell for as much as a new car. Up until 2010, before the angonoka guardians began protecting them, ploughshares had been relentlessly hunted by poachers and just a few hundred remained.

Since then, 165 rangers from 11 villages have taken turns to patrol the park each day. They use GPS trackers, radio receivers and camera equipment to monitor ploughshare numbers, and they alert the police to poachers. In 2011, angonoka guardian Henri Rakotosalama discovered two baby ploughshares, each no bigger than an adult person's thumb. It was proof that they were breeding in the wild once more.

'GREEN' TIP

Become an animal guardian by learning about endangered species where you live and telling your family and friends all about them.

CHANGING WITH THE SEASONS
TEMPERATE FORESTS

Where there are four seasons, temperate forests grow, making up a quarter of the forests on our planet. Temperate means 'not extreme', which describes the regions in between the tropics and the poles, where temperatures are mild all year round, and where these forests can be found.

Here, soil is fertile from decaying leaves and rainfall is plentiful – perfect conditions for a huge variety of plants and animals to thrive year-round. Even though winters are quiet, as many birds migrate to warmer climates and other animals hibernate from the cold, bustling life soon returns to the forest in spring.

FOUR-SEASON FORESTS

Temperate forests can be made up of deciduous trees, which lose their leaves in autumn, and coniferous trees, with tough, needle-like leaves that stay green all year long. Some temperate forests are a mix of both. Most deciduous trees are broadleaved trees, such as beech, maple, sycamore, elm and oak. Their large, flat leaves work like solar panels, absorbing sunlight and converting it into something useful – sugar to fuel their growth. As the days become shorter with the approaching winter, deciduous trees shed their leaves, channelling sugar into their roots, so they can survive until spring.

BUSTLING BROADLEAF FORESTS

With its mighty oaks and tall larches, England's Forest of Dean transforms through the year. Its dramatic autumn colours are only rivalled by the carpets of wild flowers, such as bluebells and daffodils, that light up the spring.

Spring arrives with the songs of its winged visitors returning from their winter migration: warblers warble, nightingales sing and flycatchers chirp. Yet for all the animals that migrate in winter, many more hibernate, such as hedgehogs, toads and dormice. Spring signals that it is time for these creatures to wake up.

The fresh green leaves are soft and edible for hungry fallow deer, while female foxes will hunt for rabbits and insects to feed hungry cubs in their dens. Eurasian beavers gnaw down trees to make their dams, which helps to control flooding on the River Wye, and pine martens hunt down grey squirrels.

CAN WE RISE FROM THE ASHES?

Global warming is upsetting the rhythm of the seasons by bringing forward the start of spring and making summers hotter and drier. With more sunlight, plant growing seasons are becoming longer, but with less rainfall, droughts are causing some trees to die from thirst. Droughts can spark wild fires that destroy forest habitats, already threatened by expanding towns and cities.

But thanks to our Earth Shakers, there are green shoots of hope for forest wildlife . . .

Up to 300 different insects scuttle and buzz around in the Forest of Dean. The hollowed-out trunks of old oak, beech and sweet chestnut trees are perfect nesting sites for tawny owls and lesser spotted woodpeckers.

KYRA BARBOUTIS & SOPHIE SMITH

HEDGEHOG HEROINES

Every conservation project counts, no matter how small (or prickly). Just ask cousins Kyra Barboutis and Sophie Smith who set up a hedgehog rescue centre – called Hedgehog Friendly Town – in their garden shed in Stratford-Upon-Avon, England.

In 2015, Kyra and Sophie realised that they hadn't seen a hedgehog in the garden for a long time. Hedgehog numbers have been declining across Europe at an alarming rate – it is thought only a million are left in the UK, compared to the estimated 30 million that snuffled about in the 1950s. As woodlands are cleared for houses, roads and farmland, hedgehogs and many other forest-living animals find themselves homeless. Aspiring vets Sophie and Kyra decided to do something about it.

The girls wrote letters to their neighbours, encouraging them to make holes in their fences to create 'hedgehog highways' that allow the animals to move freely through gardens in search of food or a mate. They spoke to their local vets, too, and learned how to care for hedgehogs injured on the roads, by garden tools or by pets – knowledge they put into practice back at their 'hogspital'.

"Hear that chirping sound? The little hogs are hungry! And don't underestimate how much they can poo – they're mini poo machines!"

Kyra and Sophie receive calls and messages about injured hedgehogs every day and can treat up to 45 hedgehogs at any one time. When a call for help comes in, the girls get to work and bring the hedgehog in. Caring for them involves checking for parasites such as ticks and fleas, giving medication, cleaning out their cages and hand-feeding the babies (called hoglets) every two hours. All hedgehogs are given a name when they come into the rescue centre, so that it's easy to identify them (one was named Quilliam Shakespeare after the famous playwright who was born in Stratford). Since their first rescue hedgehog, called Piglet, in 2015, Kyra and Sophie have treated and released more than 550 hedgehogs.

Rescued hoglets need to be fully grown before Kyra and Sophie can release them back into the wild.

Kyra and Sophie's work goes beyond the garden – they've visited schools across England, sharing what they've learned with children about protecting wildlife.

"If you take one thing out of a habitat, there's a knock-on effect for everything else. Imagine a habitat is a stack of wooden blocks. Take the beetle block away, something hedgehogs love to eat, and the blocks begin to wobble. Take the hedgerow block out too, and the whole thing collapses."

'GREEN' TIP

Be a nature detective and take part in backyard bird watches, butterfly counts or wildlife spotting.

(1838–1914)
JOHN MUIR
FATHER OF NATIONAL PARKS

Naturalist John Muir was born in Scotland in 1838. As a young boy, he would clamber over the craggy hills on Scotland's east coast and look out at the stormy North Sea – his love for nature had been ignited. When John was 11, his family moved to America's Midwest to become wheat farmers, leaving Scotland behind. Between many long, hard hours working on the farm, John would slip away barefoot to explore Wisconsin's wilderness, and here, John's appreciation for the natural world grew.

"People are beginning to find out that going to the mountains is going home; that wildness is a necessity; and that the mountain parks and reservations are useful not only as fountains of timber and irrigating rivers, but as fountains of life."

At the age of 29, John was temporarily blinded in an accident. The thought of never seeing nature again devastated him, so when his sight returned, John set off to explore the world. After walking 1,600 kilometres from Indiana to Florida, then sailing up America's West Coast, California's Sierra Nevada Mountains became his home.

During endless hours trekking Sierra Nevada's peaks, John became worried about how livestock were trampling and overgrazing the mountains. He began writing articles and books that celebrated nature, and petitioned the US government to protect these wild spaces as national parks.

In 1890, the US government passed bills that established John's home forests of Yosemite and Sequoia as national parks. A few years later, in 1903, one of history's most important camping trips took place. Under a tall sequoia tree in Yosemite National Park, John helped President Theodore Roosevelt shape his revolutionary conservation policies for the US to protect hundreds of wild spaces.

John Muir's legacy is the incredible National Parks of the US, but he is also a controversial figure. Muir held views that were hurtful to Black and Indigenous people – though these changed over his life. Today, the Sierra Club, which Muir co-founded, and other organisations he inspired strive for inclusivity in conservation.

'GREEN' TIP

One of the best ways to honour trees and the forest is to visit national parks. Entry fees go towards their protection.

"I wouldn't walk on the earth again until I'd done everything I possibly could to make the world aware and bring about some change."

JULIA BUTTERFLY HILL

SITTING DOWN FOR TREES

In 1996, 22-year-old Julia Butterfly Hill travelled to California to explore the ancient redwood forests. She was only meant to visit for a week, but a feeling washed over her as though she'd been pulled there for a reason. Julia discovered the forest was being cleared by a lumber company – one by one, the huge redwoods were falling.

High on a ridge, a 1,000-year-old coast redwood tree named Luna had been marked with blue paint – a sign that it was to be cut down. Julia decided then and there to take action, and for 738 days, from December 1997 to December 1999, she lived in Luna's branches.

Living under a tarpaulin on a wooden platform 50 metres up, Julia watched on as trees all around her were being cut down. The air was filled with the sound of saws, the pounding of wedges being driven into tree trunks and groans as other trees crashed to the ground. The lumber company cut off Julia's food supplies and kept her awake with floodlights, but so long as Julia sat in Luna, they couldn't chop it down.

Julia sat peacefully. She knew that if she sat up there long enough the world would take notice. Soon, her story was splashed across the news and pressure mounted on the lumber company, until, in December 1999, they at last agreed to map out a 60-metre-zone to protect Luna and the trees around it. Julia had courageously taken a stand... by sitting – and she'd won.

GREEN TIP

Almost 27,000 trees are flushed away as toilet paper every day. Use it sparingly!

WALK ON THE WILD SIDE
GRASSLANDS

Grasslands grow in 'the places in between', where there's not enough rain for forests to grow, yet too much rain for deserts to form. Just like rainforests, grasslands can be tropical or temperate depending on their location and climate.

These vast, flat landscapes blanketed with grass cover up to 40 per cent of the Earth's land and include the savannahs of Africa. At first glance, wildlife may seem sparse, but look closer and grasslands brim with biodiversity, including some of the largest land animals on the planet.

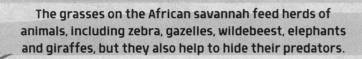

The grasses on the African savannah feed herds of animals, including zebra, gazelles, wildebeest, elephants and giraffes, but they also help to hide their predators.

TROPICAL AND TEMPERATE

The Eurasian steppe, South American pampas, South African veldts, Australia's downs and the American prairies are temperate grasslands, located north and south of the tropics. They receive around 25 to 100 centimetres of rain a year – too little for trees to grow. The tropical grasslands, or savannahs, of northern Australia, India, northern South America and East Africa experience two seasons – wet and dry. Rain falls for just a few months, before the dry season returns the savannah to drought. That's when fires ignited by lightning or people managing the land destroy the grasses' dry leaves and stems. The roots stay protected underground, ready to regrow.

THESE HOOVES WERE MADE FOR WALKING

Grasslands set the stage for some of the world's most iconic and dramatic animal migrations. When life-giving rains return to Africa's savannah, the parched earth transforms into a sea of grass once more, driving millions of hungry wildebeest and hundreds of thousands of zebra, eland and Thomson's gazelles in the Great Migration. The herds chase the rains thousands of kilometres across Kenya and Tanzania in search of good grazing grounds, while the big cats and hyenas chase the herds.

FROM GRASS TO DUST

Over thousands of years our grasslands have gradually disappeared and today it's thought that only around 10 per cent remain. We have built homes and buildings on them and used the land for farming by intensively grazing livestock and ploughing them into fields for crops. Our farms have stripped the soil of its natural goodness and disrupted nature's balance so much that many grasslands, especially in parts of Africa and Asia, have turned into lifeless, barren spaces where only dust remains.

But from the smallest bee to the mightiest beast, Earth Shakers are giving a voice to nature . . .

SELNICA OB DRAVI'S STUDENTS

BUSY BEEKEEPERS

In the small European country of Slovenia 1 in 200 people are beekeepers, or apiarists. Beekeeping is a centuries-old tradition and, here, training starts when you're very young. Budding apiarists can be found buzzing around in kindergartens and schools all over the country, nurturing colonies of the small and peaceful Carniolan honeybee.

In full bloom, Slovenia's glittering alpine meadows are bee heaven and they're dotted with painted 'bee houses' that look more like outdoor art than beehives. Inside each bee house, many hives are stacked on top of each other, each with a colourfully painted front that brings to life a traditional folk tale. The different images are intended to help the bees to identify which hive belongs to them. There are around 200,000 hives in Slovenia – some are perched on wagons that can be rolled from forests to fields, while others sit high up on city rooftops and balconies.

Just like busy worker bees, thousands of school children across the country, including those in the village of Selnica Ob Dravi, tend to school hives and special 'honey gardens', which are planted with flowers that are irresistible to their winged friends. But beekeeping goes beyond a hobby – children know that one in every three mouthfuls of food they eat depends on pollination – when bees, butterflies, beetles and wasps carry pollen from one flower to another so new plants can grow.

"No bee is no life!"

Slovenia was the first country to give its native bee protected status in 2002, before going on to ban the use of certain neonicotinoid (*nee-oh-nik-oh-tee-noyd*) insecticides, which harm bees and other pollinators, in 2011. The European Union followed Slovenia's lead by banning outdoor use of three neonicotinoids in 2018. These are steps in the right direction, but the problem for pollinators reaches beyond Europe.

'GREEN' TIP

Make your school or home bee-friendly by building a 'bee hotel' out of bricks, twigs and canes, with lots of nooks and crannies for solitary bees to nest in.

Inspired by Slovenia's centuries-old bee tradition, the UN created World Bee Day, which is celebrated on 20 May every year.

Earth gets busier every year as 140 million new people are born. With an ever-growing number of mouths to feed, crop farmers have turned to chemicals, such as insecticides, to meet demand by killing plant-eating insects. Today, 40 per cent of pollinator species, particularly bees and butterflies, face extinction and scientists worry many could vanish within this century. Many birds, frogs and reptiles survive almost entirely on an insect diet, but, with no insects to eat, those species could fast disappear too.

That's why the children at Selnica Ob Dravi have a saying: "No bee is no life!". They will tell anyone who'll listen, because our future rests on the humble bee's wings.

RACHEL CARSON
WORLD-CHANGING WORDS

In 1962, 90,000 words were about to change the world. They belonged to *Silent Spring*, a book by American nature writer and biologist Rachel Carson that was anything but silent.

During World War Two, a pesticide called DDT was used by the military to kill malaria-spreading insects and lice on soldiers, but its safeness was never tested. When the war ended, farmers and ordinary people used it for their gardens, but unlike most insecticides that destroy one or two types of insects, DDT could kill many at once.

As DDT filtered through the food chain, it killed fish and weakened birds' eggshells, threatening species, including America's national bird, the bald eagle. In 1963, just 487 breeding pairs were left. The more Rachel learned about DDT, the more she realised she could not stay silent. Rachel wrote *Silent Spring* to help stop the unchecked use of pesticides by introducing readers to the idea of ecology – that in this living world, every plant and animal is connected in a delicate web of life, including humans. She warned that all was not right in the countryside.

The chemical companies tried to discredit Rachel's book, but President Kennedy was disturbed by what he had read and immediately launched an investigation into DDT. In 1970, less than 10 years after *Silent Spring* published, the Environmental Protection Agency was set up to protect nature. One of its first acts was banning DDT in the US in 1972. Since then, bald eagle numbers have soared to more than 300,000.

'GREEN' TIP

Instead of using chemicals on your garden, homemade sprays made with oil, soap or even garlic can help deter unwanted pests.

VINCENT OPYENE
A VOICE FOR ANIMALS

'GREEN' TIP

If you're worried about a threatened species, you could adopt an animal with your pocket money – it's a great way to fund vital conservation work.

In Uganda, West Africa, extended families, called clans, are united by a totem – a sacred animal or plant that represents them, and everyone in the clan makes a promise to never, eat, hunt or harm it. The ancient tradition of totemism is one of the earliest forms of animal conservation. But in 1983, Uganda's rhinos were declared extinct in the wild, due to poaching. The black rhino was Vincent Opyene's clan totem.

Uganda is a wildlife trafficking hub, where rare and endangered animals are hunted, sold and transported to other places illegally. Sometimes live animals are smuggled as pets, but more often it's only their horns, teeth, scales or tusks that make the journey.

As a young lawyer, Vincent visited a wildlife park where wardens were losing the battle against poachers. On hearing their stories, he vowed to do something about it and he left his job to join Uganda's Wildlife Authority as a warden, patrolling the national parks. Vincent soon realised that hunters are not at the heart of the problem, wildlife traffickers are – the people who trade the illegal goods, creating an international demand.

Vincent returned to law, but this time, animal law. In 2013, he established a team of undercover investigators to track down and arrest wildlife traffickers, and, in 2017, he set up Africa's first wildlife court, allowing Vincent and the team to prosecute these criminals. The team has made over 8,000 arrests and up to 10 traffickers are put in prison each month – action that is helping to save wildlife in in Uganda.

"If an animal is hurt or killed, they don't have a family that will go to court and defend them. They needed someone who could speak for them. I am that person."

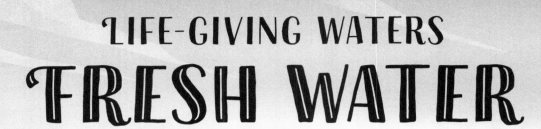

LIFE-GIVING WATERS
FRESH WATER

The big blue marble that is Earth may look full to the brim with water, but only 2.5 per cent is fresh water, and most of that is locked away in ice or underground. That leaves around one per cent of the world's fresh water in lakes, rivers and wetlands – and it's not just for fish!

Freshwater ecosystems are home to more than 100,000 plant and animal species, including birds, amphibians, reptiles, insects, mammals – and us! This biome is vital to the survival and health of every human on this planet, providing clean water to drink and wash with, and to nourish crops.

On the banks of Alaska's Brooks River, brown bears wait for their lunch. Thousands of Pacific salmon are swimming upstream from the ocean, leaping out of the water, and – when the bears are lucky – straight into their open jaws.

WORLD-SHAPING RIVERS

The world's waterways begin their journeys high in the mountains, where trickles run into streams that wind into rivers that carve the land. Rivers can be untamed giants – the longest, the Nile, snakes through 11 countries, while the mightiest, the Amazon, teems with life, including 8,000 insect species alone.

BLOOMING WONDERFUL LAKES

At their journey's end, some rivers empty into lakes. There are over 100 million lakes on Earth and Canada has more than any other country in the world. The oldest and deepest lake is Russia's Lake Baikal, which holds 20 per cent of Earth's fresh surface water. In winter its crystal-clear waters freeze over for almost five months.

WETLAND WONDERLANDS

Known as bogs, swamps, marshes, fens and ponds, wetlands cover around six per cent of Earth's land, yet 40 per cent of the world's wildlife depend on them, making them as important to biodiversity as coral reefs or rainforests. However, their reputation for being mucky and mosquito-ridden has seen many wetlands drained and built on as if they were nothing more than wastelands.

WE'RE DOWN TO OUR LAST DROP

Today, fresh water is more precious than gold. Its growing scarcity is a result of climate change, human development, increasing demand, soil erosion, and pollution from chemicals used in farming and industry. Where water once flowed freely we have built dams, where wetlands once buzzed with life we have built homes, and in many places where once there was water now there is none. With Earth's population expected to reach almost 10 billion by 2050, we are in danger of fresh water running out.

However, our freshwater habitats are not forgotten, as Earth Shakers fight to save every last drop . . .

YOLA MGOGWANA

WHEN THE TAPS RUN DRY

Twelve-year-old student and eco-warrior Yola Mgogwana is one of around two million people living outside Cape Town, South Africa's capital, in the township Khayelitsha, which means 'new town'. People here live in informal settlements and walk long distances to collect water, which has to be boiled before drinking, cooking and washing. Fresh water is hard to come by due to recurring droughts and water pollution that turns the tiny supply toxic.

The issue of taps running dry is not new for Cape Town's nearly five million residents, where the water supply comes almost entirely from rainfall captured and stored in reservoirs around the city. In mid 2018, after three years with no rain, the reservoirs were empty and Cape Town was just 90 days from Day Zero – the day when the water supply would run out. People had just 50 litres a day to live on – that's about how much goes down the toilet in five flushes. It was one of the worst droughts as a result of human-made climate change. Fortunately, the rains came and Day Zero was narrowly avoided, but in Khayelitsha the water crisis is never-ending. It's a way of life that Yola was no longer happy to accept, and so, in 2019, fed up of waiting for the adults to change things, she began marching for answers.

"How can a person live in a township where the taps run dry? My family of seven shares one communal tap with 55 families. The distance to the tap is far and the water often runs out and gets dirty, so that we can't wash our bodies, cook or flush the toilets."

Yola volunteered with the Eco Warriors club run by the Earthchild Project, where she learned about the issues affecting her community and ways she could help her school make a positive change. She shared what she'd learned with her school friends, and they began monitoring and conserving water and electricity use and set up a worm farm to make compost for the school's organic vegetable patch.

Without the club Yola says she would be in the dark about the environmental issues affecting her life. Just two months after joining Earthchild, Yola led a climate protest and bravely spoke out to over 2,000 young people. Since then, Yola has continued to share what she has learned at schools across Khayelitsha, and has called for environmental education to be part of their curriculum.

"This generation is ready for change and to bring about what is best for every single person . . . We must not stay silent anymore."

People Change not Climate Change

Try to leave EARTH a better place than when you ARRIVED

WATER IS LIFE

NO TO DAY ZERO

'GREEN' TIP

A running tap can let out up to a bucket of water each minute! So make sure you turn the tap off when you brush your teeth.

41

POORVA SHRIVASTAVA

CLEAN WATER FOR ALL

Each day in the northern Indian village of Dhulet, the women carry heavy containers back and forth to a small well that pumps water from the ground. It's back-breaking work, made impossible when the well dries up or becomes contaminated from farm chemicals. As well as unsafe water, the villagers also face a constant battle against an invasive flowering weed called *Lantana camara*, which poisons native plants and makes animals sick if they eat it. The villagers burn the weed to kill it, leaving piles of waste behind. That's when 22-year old engineering student Poorva Shrivastava had the idea to take the two problems – dirty water and plant waste – and make clean water.

Poorva took a steel drum, raised it up on bricks, drilled holes in the bottom, cut air slots into the top and inserted a pipe as a chimney. Inside, she burned coconut husks and crop waste without oxygen at temperatures so high that no smoke was released. The waste turns into solid black carbon called charcoal, which is a very effective water filter.

"The water crisis in India is hurting rural villages worst of all. Electric water filters can cost as much as a week's food and living expenses – biochar filters clean water for all."

The charcoal, which Poorva calls biochar, can be placed inside Dhulet's water tanks, filtering 3,000 litres of groundwater each day into safe drinking water. Each household in the village pays a small monthly fee to the women who operate and maintain the water tanks, providing the women with income and fresh, clean water for the village.

GREEN TIP

Collect rainwater in the garden or use leftover water from cooking to water plants.

(1953–2018)
DR ALAN RABINOWITZ

JOURNEY OF THE JAGUAR

For over 30 years, zoologist Dr Alan Rabinowitz worked to conserve the jaguar and its wild spaces – an area that stretches across 18 countries, from Argentina in South America to northern Mexico. Alan's love for this big cat began as a young boy, shortly after he developed a severe stutter. Although he struggled to speak to humans, each week Alan's father took him to the Bronx Zoo in New York, where Alan spoke freely to a jaguar.

Alan felt the world did not understand that jaguar trapped behind bars in the zoo, in the same way it did not understand that Alan's voice was trapped inside his head. Alan made a promise to himself that if he got his voice back, he would speak for the jaguar and help to save its species.

"Think about what we're giving future generations – we have to give them a world with lions and tigers and jaguars and leopards. We have to."

Jaguars roam hundreds of kilometres to hunt and find mates, using natural forest highways called 'jaguar corridors' to travel between areas. Since the mid-1800s jaguars have lost more than half of their territory to roads, canals, plantations and cattle ranches, where jaguars are often killed if they attack livestock.

Alan set up the world's first jaguar preserve in Belize in 1986, and, in 2006, co-founded Panthera, an organisation dedicated to wild-cat conservation. Panthera raises money to buy stretches of forest to protect jaguar corridors, while helping the jaguar and ranchers to peacefully coexist. In 2014, Alan led Panthera in establishing the world's largest jaguar corridor by protecting an area the size of around 14,000 football pitches in the Pantanal, a huge wetland in South America. It's now thought to be home to the highest density of jaguars anywhere on the planet.

'GREEN' TIP

You can protect threatened species where you live by joining local clean-ups that help to preserve their habitats.

THE BIG DRY
DESERTS

For every desert horizon that shimmers in the heat, there are those with sculpted dunes that twinkle with frost and snow. Deserts are places of extremes – extremely hot or extremely cold, sometimes both in one day – but all of them are extremely dry.

Deserts are found on every continent and cover around 20 per cent of Earth's land. They form where there is little moisture in the air, including in regions around the tropics, in the rain shadow of tall mountain ranges, on the western edges of continents and even at the ice caps.

PUSHING THE LIMITS

In Central Asia's remote inland desert, the Gobi, temperatures can plummet to -40 degrees Celsius in December, colder than the Arctic winter. The world's largest hot desert is the Sahara in Africa, where an average of just 75 millimetres of rain falls each year. Here, huge sandstorms can appear without warning, whipping the Sahara's nutrient-rich sands into the atmosphere and carrying them halfway around the world, where they help fertilise the Amazon.

Undeterred by the sharp spines of the towering saguaro cacti, tiny pygmy owls nest in old woodpecker holes in their woody stems.

THE SURVIVORS

At first glance, these barren landscapes may appear lifeless, but they support some of the planet's toughest wildlife, as well as one billion people. On the southwestern edge of North America lies the Sonoran Desert. It's one of the most biodiverse deserts on Earth, with around 3,500 plant, 1,000 bee, 500 bird, 100 reptile and 60 mammal species – all perfectly adapted to survive the heat.

Rattlesnakes move over the sizzling sand by raising parts of their body up and 'sidewinding'. The famously fast-running greater roadrunner can live its whole life without drinking water, by reabsorbing water from its own poo. Antelope-like pronghorns are one of the largest desert survivors. They can raise up tufts of fur to let body heat escape. Many mammals are nocturnal, such as coyotes and raccoon-like ringtails, going about their business after dark, when the temperature has cooled.

In their quest to find water, some desert plants have extra-long 'tap' roots that reach down to find pockets of water deep underground. Succulents are desert plants with thick, wax-coated leaves that seal in water and cacti, such as the prickly pear, have long, sharp spines to defend against animals keen to eat their juicy stems.

CREEPING DESERTS

As the world gets hotter and extreme droughts become more common, our deserts become even more inhospitable. Our activities are creating new deserts, too – each year an area almost as big as Greece is lost to desertification. This happens when we cut down forests on the fringes of deserts and overgraze or overwork land through farming. Land that was once fertile slowly turns to dust.

But our Earth Shakers are fighting to keep the sand at bay . . .

GUÉDÉ CHANTIER VILLAGE

HOLDING BACK THE SAND

Just below the Sahara Desert on the banks of the Doué River in Senegal, West Africa, the 7,000 villagers of Guédé Chantier make their living as fishermen, shepherds and crop farmers – but the younger generation here thinks of itself a little differently. They are Eco Sentinels determined to hold back the desert sand.

Guédé Chantier is located in the Sahel, a belt of land bridging the Sahara Desert's sands in the north and savannahs in the south. Known as the 'hunger belt', it covers 3 million square kilometres, stretching right across Africa from Senegal in the west to Eritrea in the east. Here, there are more people than there is food to feed them. Since the 1970s, droughts every few years have left millions of people without water to drink or nourish their crops. Eventually, summer monsoon rains would break the drought, making the rivers flow again, and as the Sahel sprang back to life, people returned, chopping down trees for firewood and working the delicate, sandy soil beyond what it could manage. The lands became overgrazed, overworked and – as warming temperatures kept the rains away – many areas turned to dust.

The villagers of Guédé Chantier understood that the problem they faced was not about drought, but soil. For 30 years they had grown one crop – rice – using chemical fertilisers that stripped the soil of its goodness and by 2002 little would grow. Concerned for their future, the villagers held a meeting where educator Dr Ousmane Pame spoke about ecovillages in other parts of the world, where the communities take care of the land so that it takes care of them. In 2009 Guédé Chantier was reborn as the region's first ecovillage, with its youth volunteering as 'Les Éco-sentinelles' (Eco Sentinels) to help lead the villagers towards a more sustainable life.

ECO
COMMUNE DE
GUEDE CHANTIER

The Eco Sentinels learned ways to live in harmony with nature, and led projects to collect waste, create a school garden and plant an orchard that provided both delicious fruit, and shade.

Inspired by the young Eco Sentinels, the adults began farming in a more sustainable way. Instead of planting one crop, season after season, they switched between rice, tomatoes, onion, corn and a green vegetable called okra. Each plant takes different nutrients from the ground, helping to rest the soil. The farmers learned to compost waste, harvest seeds and grow without insecticides, inspiring other villages across Africa to become eco villages too.

'GREEN' TIP

Why not speak to a teacher about starting an eco club at school? You could grow a vegetable patch or create a recycling bank.

"Thirty years ago, chemicals and pesticides were introduced to this community. But it wasn't always that way. We were once organic farmers – we are organic farmers once more, living in harmony with nature."

> "I walked all day to a well and back in Jordan's pink Arabian Desert, just so I could make a cup of tea. For the first time in my life I understood how it feels to spend the day looking for water."

MINA GULI
RUNNING DRY

Australian businesswoman Mina Guli has been fighting the water crisis with her feet. It started with a figure that stopped Mina in her tracks – 40 per cent. This is the water shortfall the world could face by 2030 – the gap between the fresh water we have and the water we need. Having experienced droughts in Australia, Mina understood how serious this was, so in 2016 she took action to bring water scarcity to the world's attention. Mina set out to run 40 marathons across seven of the planet's driest deserts in seven weeks.

Mina burned through eight pairs of trainers crossing Spain, Jordan, Antarctica, Australia, South Africa and Chile. Her supporters followed every gruelling step, pledging to save a combined 100 million litres of water by changing their everyday habits – from drinking one cup of coffee fewer a day to going meat-free one day a week (as vegetables require less water to grow than farmed animals).

But Mina's desert marathons were just a warm-up for her 2018 #RunningDry campaign – 100 marathons in 100 days, visiting some of the most water-starved communities. On day 17, as Mina ran across the Aral Sea in Uzbekistan, the extent of the water crisis truly hit home. Once one of the largest lakes in the world, the Aral Sea shrank by 90 per cent when humans changed the flow of the rivers to irrigate the land. Today, it is a rusty ship graveyard.

As Mina finished marathon 62 she broke her leg and her race was over, but then something remarkable happened... Thousands of supporters from 44 countries started donating kilometres from their own runs to help Mina reach her target. Together they ran over 800 marathons, carrying Mina's water-saving message around the world.

'GREEN' TIP

The average shower lasts 8 minutes and uses 62 litres of water – about 250 cups. Every drop counts so why not try shaving a few minutes off your shower?

(1940–2011)

WANGARI MAATHAI

THE WOMAN OF TREES

"The women here till the land, so it is important that they know how to conserve this soil."

Kenyan ecologist Wangari Maathai is the woman who planted 50 million trees across Africa. It began when she was a child, playing under the branches of a fig tree in her hometown of Nyeri. Wangari's mother would say: "That tree is the tree of God. We don't burn it. We don't cut it. We don't use it for building. We let them stand for as long as they are able to." This deep-rooted respect for nature would later help Wangari to protect it.

In 1960, 20-year-old Wangari went to university in America to study biology. Six years later she returned home, but the tree she played under as a child was gone – it had been cut down to make way for a tea plantation.

In many parts of Africa, forests were being cleared for farms and plantations. Wangari finally understood the wisdom passed down by her mother – without deep tree roots that draw water to the surface, the streams dry up and the soil washes away. Women were now walking further to source firewood, clean drinking water and food. If Wangari could help restore balance in nature, perhaps she could help empower women too?

In 1977 Wangari started the Green Belt Movement to help women grow and plant trees. The trees provided food and firewood, their roots bound the soil, and fast-growing trees could be sold, supplying a valuable income. With more than 50 million trees planted over 40 years, the Green Belt Movement lives on, transforming the landscape and people's lives.

'GREEN' TIP

Next time there's a birthday, instead of wrapping paper, try reusing gift bags or getting creative with recycled paper to wrap presents. The forests will thank you.

THE GREAT BLUE UNKNOWN
OCEANS

There is only one ocean, and it stretches around 70 per cent of Earth. In this place of constant movement great forces power life across the planet.

On the surface, currents are driven by the wind as it blows warm waters from the tropics to the poles, helping to shape the world's climate. As sunlight beams down on the ocean's surface, microscopic algae called phytoplankton bloom, releasing at least half of the world's oxygen through photosynthesis, and warm surface waters evaporate and condense to form clouds that carry life-giving rain across the planet. Near the poles, cold, nutrient-rich waters sink to the bottom of the ocean, where deep-ocean currents flow like rivers and carry them across the globe. From food and water to the air that we breathe, it is clear that our health is connected to the ocean in a way that cannot be broken.

In the warm shallow waters off Hawaii, grey reef sharks patrol the corals, feasting on fish, jellyfish and octopuses.

DIVING INTO THE DEPTHS

In the Pacific Ocean, in the sun-dappled shadows of the sunlight zone, green sea turtles come up for air as colourful reef fish dart in and out of the coral cities below. Glimmering schools of fish, such as anchovies, scatter as gannets dive beneath the waves and sailfish slice through the water chasing their next meal.

Between 200 and 1,000 metres down, in the twilight zone, plants disappear, along with light and warmth. Microscopic animals and newly hatched fish and crustaceans, such as crabs and lobsters, are known as zooplankton. Along with other animals, including bioluminescent lanternfish, zooplankton spend their time travelling up to the surface at night to feed on phytoplankton, before returning to the deep.

No sunlight reaches beyond 1,000 metres, marking the start of the midnight zone. Giant squid as long as lorries try to outswim sperm whales longer than buses. The deeper you go, the greater the weight of the ocean pressing down. At a depth of 4,000 metres, the bone-crushing abyssal zone begins, where marine arthropods, such as sea spiders, stride across the muddy floor, sucking life from their prey. Huge cracks in the ocean floor give way to deep-sea trenches that plunge into the deepest unknowns.

IN DEEP WATER

The beautiful blue is being overused and under-protected. Every minute, enough plastic to fill a rubbish truck is dumped into the ocean; many inhabitants, from whales to sharks, have been hunted to the brink of extinction and warming ocean temperatures are damaging our coral reefs, one of the planet's most exquisite natural wonders.

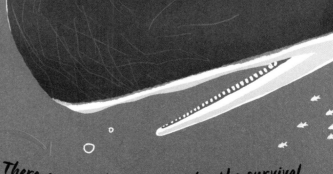

There are rough seas ahead for the survival of our oceans, but, unafraid, our Earth Shakers are steering into the storm . . .

51

MELATI & ISABEL WIJSEN
BYE BYE PLASTIC BAGS

In the Indian Ocean there's an emerald island where jungled hills dip their toes into the sea, ancient temples are surrounded by rice terraces, and as far as the eye can see there is... plastic! Every day on the Indonesian island of Bali, enough plastic to fill a 14-storey building is thrown away, and it makes its way into drains, rivers and, finally, the ocean. The beautiful beaches have become bottle- and bag-strewn and Indonesia has become the world's second biggest plastic polluter, after China. But in 2013, the tide began to change as sisters Melati and Isabel Wijsen (then aged 10 and 12) decided to reclaim their island by saying goodbye to plastic bags.

Eight million tonnes of plastic – an amount heavier than the Great Pyramid of Giza – enters the ocean every year. It breaks down into tiny pieces, known as microplastics, and gets swallowed by many animals, including filter-feeders such as whales. All over the ocean, animals – such as turtles – mistakenly eat plastic bags thinking they're jellyfish, seabirds – such as albatrosses – take floating plastic back to their nests to feed to their chicks, and creatures – such as seals – get trapped in abandoned fishing nets, known as ghost nets, which are virtually invisible in the water.

At school, Melati and Isabel were learning about inspirational people, such as South Africa's first black president Nelson Mandela, American civil rights activist Martin Luther King, and Princess Diana, who campaigned to ban landmines. People who helped change the world by fighting for what they believed in. Melati and Isabel wanted to change their corner of the world too, but how? As the tide lapped at their ankles, the answer lay tangled at their feet – plastic. Melati and Isabel set up Bye Bye Plastic Bags, a youth-led organisation to help tackle Bali's plastic problem.

"Young people from all over Bali joined our clean-up crew as we cleaned up plastic piling up in the rivers and rice fields and clogging up gutters in our streets. On one day alone, 12,000 people helped us gather up 43 tonnes of garbage."

In 2014, Melati and Isabel's hard work was noticed by the governor of Bali, who asked to meet with them. The governor swore to ban plastic bags on the island, a promise kept when the new governor signed a law to ban them in 2019. Six years after Melati and Isabel started their campaign, Bali finally said BYE BYE to plastic bags.

"Kids have the power to do things. You don't need a business plan or a hidden agenda, it all starts with an idea and a group of friends. Any kids reading this who want to do something – GO FOR IT! It's not going to be easy, sometimes it'll be really hard. But believe us, it'll be worth it."

GREEN TIP

You can ban the bag, too, by buying a reusable tote bag that you can decorate and use again and again.

DR AYANA ELIZABETH JOHNSON

VIP (VERY IMPORTANT PARROTFISH)

Brooklyn-born Dr Ayana Elizabeth Johnson first fell in love with coral reefs as a five-year-old on holiday in Florida. As she stared through the floor of a glass bottom boat, a magical underwater world revealed itself, and Ayana decided she wanted to become a marine biologist. Twenty-five years later, while studying coral reefs in the Caribbean, Ayana fell in love all over again... this time, with a fabulously flamboyant fish.

With a beak full of tough teeth, parrotfish are critical to the health of the reef. Like underwater lawnmowers, they constantly graze on the furry algae that grows on the reef and this helps the coral to grow. Unfortunately, in the Caribbean communities of Curaçao and Bonaire, the local fishermen's nets and traps were unintentionally scooping up small parrotfish, which caused their numbers to decline. In turn, the reef became overwhelmed by algae.

"Over 500 fish species live on Caribbean reefs, but the ones I just can't get out of my head are parrotfish."

From 2007 to 2016, Ayana began counting the fish and working with Caribbean fishermen to protect these VIPs – Very Important Parrotfish. Together, Ayana and the fishermen redesigned fish traps to reduce by-catch – the fish they did not set out to catch – by 80 per cent, and Ayana's findings helped to give parrotfish protected status in many parts of the Caribbean. On the island of Barbuda, Ayana helped set up safe spots in the sea that are protected from overfishing. These have now been adopted across other Caribbean islands, helping locals continue to safely use the sea's resources... without using them all up.

'GREEN' TIP

We can all support ocean biodiversity by checking the packaging on foods we buy that come from the sea, to ensure they have been caught or farmed in a sustainable way.

ERICH HOYT

SAVING A WHALE CALLED KILLER

Fast-swimming pack-hunters with big appetites, orcas have earned the reputation of being 'killers', and over many decades they have been shot at by fishermen or captured to live in aquariums. However, Canadian-American marine conservationist Erich Hoyt has dedicated his life to protecting whales and dolphins and their ocean homes.

In 1973, on a boat in Canada's Robson Bight – a bay that annually attracts one of the largest concentration of orcas on the planet, 23-year-old Erich began working with researchers on the world's first wild orca study. Over seven summers, as the orcas visited the bay on their migration to the Arctic, Erich learned to identify each one by its dorsal fin, including a curious female called Stubbs, and soon discovered why this bay was so special to them. The orcas would swim into the shallows of the bay and rub their bodies along the smooth, thumb-sized pebbles. There was no other place like it anywhere on their travels.

In the late 1970s a logging company was given permission to cut down the trees on the slopes above the bay. Logs were going to be floated downriver into the bay, crowding the orcas' rubbing beaches. Concerned that the orcas would be driven away, Erich and his friends campaigned for two years, until, in 1982, the government finally set aside Robson Bight as an ecological reserve.

"The Battle of Robson Bight set a course for my life, mapping the entire ocean to discover where the important areas are for marine mammals so that we have a fighting chance of protecting them."

When Erich returned to Robson Bight in 2010 Stubbs' pod was there – her descendants, including several whales Erich had first met more than 30 years before. By protecting the rubbing beaches, Erich had helped preserve this important place for generations of orcas to come.

'GREEN' TIP

You can help protect whales and dolphins by always remembering that the ocean is their home and we are just visiting. Be sure to take your rubbish home when you leave the beach.

POLES APART
ICE WORLDS

There are still places in this world barely touched by humans. The Arctic lies at Earth's northernmost end, a frozen sea surrounded by land. Its polar opposite in Antarctica is a frozen continent surrounded by sea.

For six months of the year, the Sun doesn't rise at the poles, and the Arctic and Antarctica take turns remaining in darkness. With little sunlight, chilly temperatures and limited fresh water, these ice worlds are the planet's harshest habitats, testing the very limits of life's ability to survive.

LIFE IN THE WHITE WILDERNESS

In the lower latitudes of the Arctic, in areas known as tundra, hundreds of species of low-growing plants can be found, but on even colder Antarctica there is so much ice that only a scattering of lichen, moss and fungi grow. With so little to eat, very few animals can live on the land. Instead, the water teems with life. Marine creatures – from narwhals and seals in the Arctic to whales and seabirds in Antarctica – migrate across the ocean to the polar regions to feast on swarms of tiny crustaceans called krill, which look like huge balls of pink candyfloss. The krill are a small but vital link in the food chain.

Temperatures in the Arctic can plunge to around -50 degrees Celsius – nearly three times as frosty as your freezer.

WINTER WARRIORS

To survive in polar regions, animals need unbeatable winter wardrobes. The Arctic fox's thick fur changes with the season – from snow-white in winter to grey in summer, to match the bare rocks – so that it can sneak up on its prey. Arctic wolves have two layers of fur: a soft, warm undercoat and longer guard hairs that act like a raincoat. Appearing to wear socks, the snowshoe hare's enormous feet are like snowshoes, allowing it to walk on top of the snow.

Like many polar mammals, the polar bear has thick skin and an even thicker layer of fat, called blubber, to store its energy reserves. This keeps it warm as it heads out on the sea ice to catch seals. Also hunting seals, orcas work together using the tactic of creating waves, which wash seals off the ice.

ON THIN ICE

As the planet gets warmer, sea ice is shrinking, leaving behind dark water that absorbs heat, rather than white ice that reflects the Sun's rays, helping to keep our planet cool. As the Arctic and Antarctic are warming faster than the global average, its animal inhabitants are finding it harder to adapt quickly enough to survive. Melting sea ice leaves polar bears without a platform to hunt from, forcing them to swim longer distances to find ice or return to land. The more ice that melts, the higher sea levels rise, threatening coastal habitats and communities.

The health of our planet is on thin ice, but our Earth Shakers are determined to stop it from melting . . .

CLIMATE STRIKE KIDS

FRIDAYS FOR FUTURE

It began in Sweden, Stockholm, in 2018, with a 15-year-old girl in a yellow raincoat called Greta Thunberg. An unusually hot and dry summer had ignited wildfires around the world – from Greta's home city of Stockholm and countries across Europe to California in the US. It was clear to Greta that because of human-made climate change… "our house is on fire."

On 20 August 2018, instead of going to school, Greta sat down on the pavement outside Sweden's Riksdag (parliament) demanding her government take action on the climate crisis. She returned week after week, holding four words that would start a revolution: School Strike for Climate.

Those four words spread like the wildfires. People joined Greta on the pavement, journalists began to tell her story and the hashtag #SchoolStrike4Climate carried Greta's protest around the planet. Fridays now belonged to the students as they took to the streets demanding climate action. #FridaysForFuture was born.

The Fridays For Future youth movement is calling for governments to move away from fossil fuels and invest in renewable energies – clean power from the Sun, wind, water and heat – to reduce carbon emissions and help keep the global temperature increase below 1.5 degrees Celsius. This will help prevent future rising sea levels and more extreme weather events.

"What do we want?
Climate action!
When do we want it?
NOW!"

A year after her first strike, Greta inspired 7.6 million people in 185 countries to take a stand with Fridays For Future. In 2019, more than 11,000 scientists from 153 countries added their voices to the movement when they declared a 'climate emergency'. At the same time, the European Union urged all of its countries to commit to net zero emissions by 2050, so that the total amount of greenhouse gases put into the atmosphere would be balanced by the amount taken out naturally by forests, wetlands and other ecosystems, or captured through new technologies.

'GREEN' TIP

You're never too young to make your voice heard. Write a letter or an email telling your country's leaders how climate change is affecting you.

Although thousands of kilometres apart, in 2018 millions of young people in towns and cities across the planet came together as a single voice calling for climate action.

SAVE THE PLANET

As many countries make progress in reducing their emissions, others continue to expand their fossil fuel industries and reject climate science. Fearless in her mission, Greta set sail to meet them on a carbon-neutral journey across the Atlantic Ocean from Plymouth, England, to the 2019 Climate Summit in New York, America. Her message was clear...

———

"The eyes of all future generations are upon you. And if you choose to fail us, I say we will never forgive you. We will not let you get away with this. Right here, right now is where we draw the line. The world is waking up. And change is coming, whether you like it or not."

———

THERE IS NO 🌍 PLANET B

OUR PLANET OUR FUTURE

SKOLSTREJK FÖR KLIMATET

The sea is RISING and so are WE

SCHOOL STRIKE FOR CLIMATE ACTION

WILL STEGER
ON THIN ICE

In 1959, inspired by Huckleberry Finn's adventures on the Mississippi River in Mark Twain's stories, then 15-year-old Will Steger used his savings to buy a motorboat and take the trip himself. Years later, Will's appetite for adventure led him to embark on some of the world's most significant expeditions in the name of conservation.

In 1989, Will set off on the first and longest unsupported dog sled journey across Antarctica. It would test the limits of human endurance for 222 days across 5,500 kilometres, but the aim was to protect Antarctica.

"Of everything I've ever done, it was my most important expedition – an epic adventure that had real purpose. I needed to make Antarctica famous, so I could help save it."

The Antarctic Treaty, an international agreement between 12 countries to preserve Antarctica, had been in place for 30 years, but did not include a ban on mining. As time had passed, more countries wanted to explore the icy continent for its underground mineral resources. Antarctica's ice sheet helps to keep our planet cool, and the surrounding Southern Ocean absorbs vast amounts of CO_2. Disrupting nature's balance here would be disastrous.

On his return from the Antarctic crossing in 1990, Will visited world leaders asking them to revise the Antarctic Treaty to include a mining ban. They listened, and 48 countries agreed to protect Antarctica as a nature reserve. Will had succeeded, but his work was far from over.

Today, Will informs thousands of global educators on how to teach their students about climate change. And he never stops exploring, bringing back vital eyewitness accounts of how warming is altering unseen corners of our planet.

'GREEN' TIP
A carbon calculator can help you measure your 'carbon footprint' and consider ways to tread more lightly on the planet.

PREM GILL

STUDYING SEALS FROM SPACE

Polar conservationist Prem Gill, also known as Polar Prem, grew up in a working-class Punjabi family, never imagining he could have a career as a polar explorer. Unlike a traditional explorer, Prem uses the power of satellite technology, and studies Antarctic seals… from space!

Using satellite cameras, Prem zooms in on satellite images until he can make out the distinctive banana shapes of Antarctic seals resting on the ice. By counting the seals and discovering where they give birth or what type of sea ice they live on, Prem helps conservationists understand which areas of sea ice to protect.

"I love exploring these 'hidden worlds' and knowing that I'm possibly the only human to have ever seen this remote side of nature."

In early 2020, Prem arrived in Antarctica where he spent two weeks balancing in a boat, holding a long stick with a sensor called a 'field spectrometer'. The spectrometer measures light wavelengths reflected off different seal species, which allowed Prem to identify them in satellite images.

Studying Antarctic seals in the field is hugely challenging – the region is remote, broken pack ice makes it dangerous to reach by boat, and it's so vast it's impossible to explore by plane – which makes Prem's work gathering this data so vital for conservation. It helps scientists protect the seals' wild habitats, ensuring a brighter future for their species.

'GREEN' TIP

Visit the British Antarctic Survey online at www.bas.ac.uk to discover more about how scientists help to preserve the poles.

MORE EARTH SHAKERS

Every day, more and more people become Earth Shakers, standing up for nature and our future. Here are some more of their stories.

ROMARIO VALENTINE

Cleaning up beaches in South Africa

When Romario Valentine was six, he was asked to be an orca in his school play. As Romario researched orcas and the ocean, it ignited his interest in wildlife. Since 2017, Romario has led more than 150 beach clean-ups to help protect the ocean, and on his ninth birthday, instead of a party and presents, he asked for donations to a nearby endangered bird sanctuary. Through his fundraising and beautiful bird paintings, Romario has helped teach children around the world about conservation.

DARA MCANULTY

Saving wildlife with words

The noisy human-made world can be an overwhelming place for Dara McAnulty, who has autism. In 2016, 16-year-old Dara started a blog about nature called 'Naturalist Dara', which helped to drown out the noise of the busy world. Dara shared his adventures of rescuing bats, recording red squirrel sightings and monitoring the rare hen harrier, which is facing extinction. Dara's conservation work and nature writing has earned him many awards and roles as an ambassador for the RSPCA and the Jane Goodall Institute. In 2020, he had his first book published, which celebrates the beauty of nature.

NEMONTE NENQUIMO

Activist in the Amazon

Nemonte Nenquimo is a leader of the indigenous Waorani people of the Amazon rainforest of Ecuador. Since her community were first contacted by people from the outside world in the 1950s they have struggled to protect their forest home from logging, human settlement and oil exploration. In 2019 the Ecuadorian government announced it was going to auction off Waorani land to the oil industry's highest bidder, so Nemonte and the Waorani took a stand. Nemonte went to court and won a landmark victory to protect 500,000 acres of Waorani rainforest (an area bigger than London), setting a precedent for other communities in the Amazon.

JOHN FRANCIS

The Planet Walker

In 1971, two oil tankers collided in San Francisco Bay, spilling around 800,000 gallons of oil into the sea – more than you could hold in an Olympic swimming pool. As 25-year-old John Francis scrubbed beaches and fought to save oil-soaked wildlife, he decided to make a bigger change in his own life – to give up driving and riding in motor vehicles powered by oil. For 22 years John walked to get around, even walking across North America, from the west coast to the east coast. John has helped to write oil spill regulations to protect America's blue spaces and is now a United Nations Goodwill Ambassador, drawing the world's attention to the UN's conservation work.

PARAG DEKA

Standing up for the little guys

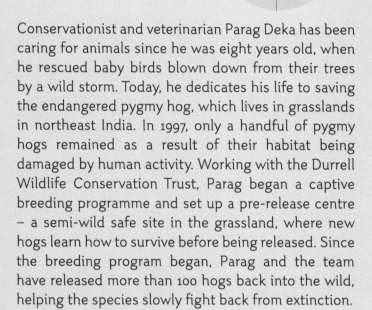

Conservationist and veterinarian Parag Deka has been caring for animals since he was eight years old, when he rescued baby birds blown down from their trees by a wild storm. Today, he dedicates his life to saving the endangered pygmy hog, which lives in grasslands in northeast India. In 1997, only a handful of pygmy hogs remained as a result of their habitat being damaged by human activity. Working with the Durrell Wildlife Conservation Trust, Parag began a captive breeding programme and set up a pre-release centre – a semi-wild safe site in the grassland, where new hogs learn how to survive before being released. Since the breeding program began, Parag and the team have released more than 100 hogs back into the wild, helping the species slowly fight back from extinction.

BOYAN SLAT

Fighting plastic with technology

During a scuba diving trip in Greece at the age of 16, Boyan Slat was shocked to see more plastic than fish and was surprised to learn that nobody had attempted to tackle the ocean plastic problem. So, in 2013, he quit studying aerospace engineering to develop the world's first ocean clean-up system. Five years later, it launched from San Francisco Bay, off the west coast of the US. Using 600 metres of pipe, Boyan created a U-shaped floating boom that glides with the current, gathering up plastic. Once the boom has collected as much as it can hold – anything from one-tonne ghost nets to tiny microplastics – a boat transports the rubbish into shore for recycling. Boyan hopes his invention can clean up 90 per cent of the Great Pacific Garbage Patch by 2040.

AABID SURTI

Turning off the taps in India

Since 2007, grandfather Aabid Surti has gone door-to-door in Mumbai, India, fixing leaking taps for free. Aabid was all too aware of the importance of water conservation – he grew up seeing his mother queue to get water from a pump. After reading a newspaper report that said a leaky tap could waste 1,000 litres of water each month, Aabid set up his organisation – The Drop Dead Foundation. He believes he has helped to save more than 20 million litres of water – enough to fill eight Olympic swimming pools.

CALLIE BROADDUS

Saving cloud forests in Ecuador

In 2019, then 28-year-old Callie Broaddus set up Reserva: the Youth Land Trust, hoping to create the world's first entirely youth-funded nature reserve. With support from the Rainforest Trust, Ecuadorian conservation group the EcoMinga Foundation and young people around the world, Reserva reached their first fundraising goal of $178,296 in 2021, to fund a 244-acre site in the Chocó cloud forest of Ecuador. This will allow them to expand an existing nature reserve and protect rainforest from farming and development.

10 SMALL CHANGES FOR A BIG DIFFERENCE

There are lots of incredible things we can do when we think SMALL and they can make a positive difference in the world. This book has already included lots of green tips, and here are 10 that you, your friends and your family can put into action today.

1. Turn food waste into soil

Throw food scraps, such as fruit and vegetable peelings, into a compost bin in the garden. It will slowly transform into soil that's great for growing new plants in.

2. Give 'rubbish' a second chance

Reuse shopping bags, water bottles and scrap paper. If something is broken try mending it, or if it is now unwanted, give it to friends or to charity, so that someone else can use it.

3. Take charge of the recycling at home

Sort glass, tin cans, plastic and paper, and put them into the recycling bin. This gives them a second life as new products and keeps them out of landfill.

4. Slay energy vampires

Unplug phone chargers and game consoles that drain electricity, even when they're not in use.

5. Go wild

It's easy to turn a corner of your garden into a pollinator paradise. Let the grass get tall and allow weeds, such as dandelions and clover, to grow. They're food sources for many insects.

6. Use your legs

Biking or walking about 1.5 kilometres a day for a year (instead of taking the car) could stop almost 150 kilograms of CO_2 from entering the atmosphere. It's as effective as planting four trees and letting them grow for 10 years!

7. Try a meatless Monday

Meat farming produces a lot of greenhouse gases compared to other foods, so why not try a plant-based meal once a week to reduce your carbon footprint?

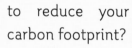

8. Swot up

Borrow books from your local library to learn more about Earth Shakers and nature. It's completely free and a great place to start for sharing ideas and information with your family, friends, teachers and neighbours.

9. Eat local

From local honey and vegetables to bread, eggs and milk, lots of essential foods are probably grown or produced near you. Buying from local shops and sellers helps reduce greenhouse gas emissions, because these products don't have to travel far to reach you.

10. And remember to be kind

Take care of the natural world and the plants and animals that live here. Remember, it's their home too.

DISCOVER MORE

Learning more about our planet, the incredible wildlife that calls it home and the amazing people who are helping to protect it has never been easier. Not only is it fascinating, but it will help you to make more planet-friendly choices now and in the future. Here are some useful resources for finding out more. Plus, there's lots of ways to get involved with the Earth Shakers in this book, too.

MORE ON EARTH SHAKER PROJECTS

Nepalese Youth for Climate Action www.nyca.net.np
Find out more about how young people are standing up to air pollution in Nepal.

The Durrell Wildlife Conservation Trust www.durrell.org
Learn about programmes to protect species, including the mountain chicken frog, ploughshare tortoise and many more.

Plant for the Planet www.plantfortheplanet.org
Plant or pledge trees to support the global Trillion Tree Campaign.

Frankfurt Zoological Society's Jungle School, Sumatra
https://sumatra.fzs.org/en/orang-utan-conservation/orangutan-rehabilitation-jungle-school
Meet the Jungle School orangutans and find out more about their school day.

Hedgehog Friendly Town www.hedgehogfriendlytown.co.uk
Find out the latest hedgehog rescue centre news and how you can help hedgehogs.

Panthera www.panthera.org
Learn more about big cat conservation all over the world.

The Global Eco Village Network www.ecovillage.org
Discover the eco villages across the world that are becoming more sustainable.

The Green Belt Movement www.greenbeltmovement.org
Support GBM projects in Kenya and find out how you can get involved in your neighbourhood.

Bye Bye Plastic Bags Campaign www.byebyeplasticbags.org
Find the BBPB team nearest to you and learn how you can help the ban the bag.

Ocean Cleanup Project www.theoceancleanup.com
Help fund the Ocean Cleanup by buying sunglasses made from plastic scooped from the sea.

Climate Generation www.climategen.org

Set up by Will Steger, with resources to support your climate action.

Fridays For Future www.fridaysforfuture.org

To find out why, how and where to strike for climate action.

Reserva: The Youth Land Trust www.reservaylt.org

Discover how writing a letter can help save the rainforest.

Jane Goodall's Roots and Shoots www.rootsnshoots.org.uk

Find out how to make positive changes for people, animals and the environment.

Sea Shepherd www.seashepherd.org.au

Learn more about the fight to defend sharks in our ocean.

 ## WATCH LIST

TED (which stands for 'Technology, Entertainment and Design') is a non-profit organisation dedicated to spreading ideas and knowledge, usually in the form of video talks up to 18 minutes long. They are inspiring, challenging and thought-provoking, and a great way to learn from other people. Many of the Earth Shakers in this book have given TED talks – and they are not the only ones. You can search for them at **www.ted.com**

Look out for talks by: Greta Thunberg, Melati and Isabel Wijsen, Boyan Slat, Ayana Elizabeth Johnson, John Francis, Aabid Surti, Al Gore – American politician and environmentalist, and Jane Goodall – English primatologist and conservationist.

 ## STUDY

This book includes zoologists, marine biologists, researchers, climatologists, veterinarians, activists, teachers and more! If you'd like to do a job that helps protect the planet too, then now is a good time to start thinking about it. Here are a few subjects that might be useful in your future studies:

- Biology
- Chemistry
- Climatology
- Conservation science
- Ecology
- Environmental engineering
- Geology
- Marine biology
- Meteorology
- Oceanography
- Sustainability
- Urban planning

 ## VOLUNTEER

Until then, you can volunteer for a wildlife conservation organisation or with a litter clean-up near you. It's a great way to gain experience, meet people that care about the environment, and learn about nature.

Beach Clean
9AM Sunday

17

24

31

GLOSSARY

AIR POLLUTION – harmful particles in the air, such as those released in car exhaust fumes and factory emissions.

ATMOSPHERE – the layer of gases surrounding Earth.

BIOME – a large region of Earth that has a certain climate and certain types of wildlife that live there. Major biomes include rainforests, grasslands and deserts.

BIODIVERSITY – the variety of life on Earth.

CARBON DIOXIDE – a colourless and odourless gas that occurs in Earth's atmosphere. There is a small amount of it in the air we exhale, and large amounts in the emissions from factories and vehicles.

CARBON FOOTPRINT – the amount of greenhouse gas emissions produced by the activities of someone or something.

CLIMATE CHANGE – the change in Earth's average climate conditions, such as temperature and rainfall, over a long period.

CLIMATE SUMMIT – a meeting between world leaders to combat climate change.

CONSERVATION – protecting the natural world and the wildlife that lives in it.

DEFORESTATION – when forests are cut down, often to make room for crop farms, cattle ranches or the expansion of towns and cities, without being replanted.

DESERT – a dry area of land that receives no more than 25 centimetres of rainfall a year.

DESERTIFICATION – when fertile land becomes dry, losing vegetation and wildlife, and gradually turns into desert.

EARTH SHAKERS – people all around the world who are taking action to protect our planet.

ECOLOGY – the study of how organisms interact with one another and their environment.

ECOSYSTEM – a community of plants, animals and other living organisms that interact with each other in an environment.

EMISSIONS – the release of greenhouse gases into the air, contributing to global warming and climate change.

ENVIRONMENT – the surroundings that a person, plant or animal lives in.

EROSION – when wind, water and ice wear away soil and rock, moving it from one location to another. Gravity can cause erosion, too.

EUROPEAN UNION – a union of 27 European countries, whose aim is to foster peace and encourage political and economic cooperation.

FOOD CHAIN – the connection between living things, which shows who eats who to survive.

FOSSIL FUELS – substances found in the Earth's crust, formed from ancient decomposing plants and animals, that are extracted and burned to make energy. They include oil, gas and coal.

GLACIER – a slow-moving river of ice found on high mountains and near the poles.

GLOBAL WARMING – the gradual increase in the average temperature of Earth's atmosphere as a result of increased levels of greenhouse gases.

HABITAT – the home environment of plants, animals or other organisms.

METHANE – a colourless and odourless natural gas that is produced by wetlands, cows and landfill sites.

MICROPLASTICS – tiny, glitter-sized plastic pieces that make their way into the ocean and freshwater habitats, threatening wildlife.

OZONE LAYER – A thin layer high up in the atmosphere that helps protect us by absorbing harmful ultraviolet rays that can burn our skin.

POACHER – someone who illegally hunts, kills or traps an animal to sell it or its body parts (such as horns or tusks).

POLE – the northernmost or southernmost point on Earth's axis.

POLLUTION – the introduction of noise, heat, light, chemicals, gases or human waste that contaminates a natural environment.

RAINFOREST – a warm forest habitat found near the equator that receives more than 2 metres of rainfall a year.

RECYCLE – turning waste, such as paper, cans and plastic, into new materials.

RENEWABLE ENERGY – energy generated from sources, such as sunlight, wind and waves, which can be used again and again without running out.

SMOG – polluted air that settles over cities, primarily caused by vehicle emissions or the burning of fossil fuels.

SUSTAINABILITY – when people use resources, such as wood, water and fish, in a balanced way – taking what they need without harming the natural world, and leaving enough for future generations.

TEMPERATE FOREST – a forest that experiences four seasons, found in regions between the tropics and the poles.

TRAFFICKING – when endangered or protected animals (or their body parts) are illegally hunted, sold and transported to other places.

UNITED NATIONS – an organisation of many of the world's countries who agree to work together to promote peace and find solutions to the world's biggest problems.

A LETTER FROM THE AUTHOR

I'm very lucky to have grown up on Australia's east coast, by the Great Barrier Reef, being visited by nesting marine turtles, migrating humpback whales and, best of all, sharks – from hammerheads and reef sharks to the majestic tiger shark.

In the Australian winter of 2018, I sat on the shore in my hometown of Bundaberg, Queensland, staring out at the twinkling sea. On that day, I watched a man in a small boat go out to a floating orange buoy called a drum line. What I couldn't see below the surface was that a large, baited hook was dangling in the water to lure and trap sharks. When the man pulled up the line, he found that a tiger shark had been hooked... and drowned. I was horrified. The idea of killing sharks so we can swim at the beach seemed as ludicrous to me as shooting lions so we can picnic on Africa's Serengeti grasslands. More and more, I became heartbroken by the terrible things happening in nature. But how could someone like me make a difference? I wasn't a scientist, I hadn't invented anything, and it seemed unlikely I'd meet the Prime Minister anytime soon. But there was one thing I could do.

I could write.

I had an idea to write this book, giving a voice to nature and the many unsung heroes tirelessly working to protect it. I got to work, visiting and phoning scientists, explorers, activists, inventors and conservationists. I thought of them as Earth Shakers, and as we spoke, I learned that our world is getting hotter and drier, that our weather is getting wilder, that the sea is getting higher, and that more and more extinctions will happen in my lifetime. About 30 hours of interviews later, and, with the help of incredible illustrator Lydia Hill and my editor Carly Blake, a book began to take shape. We were becoming Earth Shakers too. Will you join us?

You're not too small. You're not unimportant. You can be an Earth Shaker – a force of nature that's good in the world. It starts by understanding how everything we do has an environmental cost – from the meals we eat, and the way we travel, to switching on a light each night. Being mindful of our individual footprint on the world and being willing to make changes is the first step in changing our future. However small at first, it all counts. We have too much at stake not to try. This is, after all, an altogether wonderful place to call home.

Leisa Stewart-Sharpe

ABOUT THE ILLUSTRATOR

Lydia Hill is a British illustrator who graduated from Middlesex University in London. Since leaving university, Lydia has continued to develop her light-hearted and vibrant art style, working on two non-fiction children's picture books and a range of projects including editorial and branding.

Lydia's work aims to inject fun into everyday life by focusing on diverse and quirky characters in colourful natural scenes, and hopes to connect young readers to stories that inspire them to cherish the natural world. She currently lives in Sheffield, England.